D0190361

**24 Hour Telephone Renewals 020 8489 4560**

**HARINGEY LIBRARIES**

THIS BOOK MUST BE RETURNED ON OR BEFORE
THE LAST DATE MARKED BELOW

Alexandra Park Library

To          Alexandra Park Rd N22 7UJ

70001413785 6

| HARINGEY PUBLIC LIBRARY | |
|---|---|
| 70001413785 6 | |
| PETERS | 29-Mar-2018 |
| £11.99 | |
| | |

Jane Clarke & Britta Teckentrup

# FIREFLY
# HOME

nosy
crow

**There's no place like home,**
and this special place is home for . . . fireflies.

Fireflies have a bright light inside
them that shimmers and shines.

But, wait! One little firefly is missing . . .

Here she is, all by herself.
Her name is **Florence.** Say, "Hello, Florence!"

But poor Florence looks very sad.
Do you think she is **lost?** Let's see if
we can help her find her way home.

But where shall we start?
Oh, look! There's a bright **light**
peeping through the trees.
Could that be home?
Let's turn the page and see.

No, that's not home. It's just the big, bright
**moon** above the sparkling sea.
Never mind.

What about those **flashes** of light over there?
Could that be home?

No, that's not home. It's just a **lighthouse**
shining out to the boats bobbing on the water.

Now Florence has spotted
a **long line** of moving lights.
Could **that** be home?

No, **that's** not home. It's just a **train** whizzing down the track.

But the train's lights are so **pretty** that
Florence wants to follow them.

Say, "Fly faster, Florence!"
and flap your hands to show
her how to fly really **fast . . .**

That **was** fast!
And, look! Where are we now?

We're in the **big city,** and there
are bright lights **everywhere.**
But is it home?

**No!** This isn't where fireflies live.
These lights are **too bright!**

And where's Florence?
She's **lost** again.
Can you **point** to her?

Yes, **there** she is!
Let's quickly turn the page
to help her fly away.

That's better.
This park is lovely and calm.
But poor Florence still looks very sad.
She **really** needs to find
her way home.

Perhaps we need
to **make a wish . . .**

Let's wish on a **shooting star!**
There are **lots** of shooting stars here.

Close your eyes and wish
**very hard** that Florence will
find her way home soon . . .

Wait!
Are they **really** shooting stars?

**No!** They're . . .

# . . . fireflies!

**They** will know the way home!
Trace the bright firefly trails with your
finger, and say, "Fly, Florence, fly!"
to help her follow them . . .

**. . . all the way home!**

Your wish has come true!
Florence is **so** happy to be home
at last with all her firefly friends.

Whisper, "Night, night, Florence!"
and blow her a goodnight kiss.

**Goodnight!**

For Elowyn, who was a
tiny glimmer when we
watched the fireflies
— J.C.

For Hajo — B.T.

First published 2018
by Nosy Crow Ltd
The Crow's Nest, 14 Baden Place
Crosby Row, London SE1 1YW
www.nosycrow.com

ISBN 978 1 78800 023 9

Nosy Crow and associated logos
are trademarks and/or
registered trademarks of
Nosy Crow Ltd

Text © Jane Clarke 2018
Illustrations © Britta Teckentrup 2018

The right of Jane Clarke to be identified
as the author of this work and of Britta Teckentrup
to be identified as the illustrator of this work
has been asserted.

All rights reserved

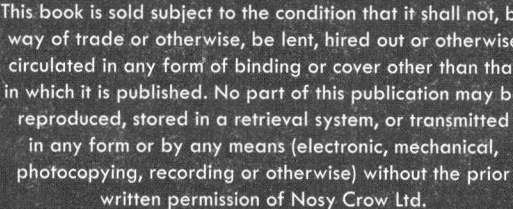

This book is sold subject to the condition that it shall not, by
way of trade or otherwise, be lent, hired out or otherwise
circulated in any form of binding or cover other than that
in which it is published. No part of this publication may be
reproduced, stored in a retrieval system, or transmitted
in any form or by any means (electronic, mechanical,
photocopying, recording or otherwise) without the prior
written permission of Nosy Crow Ltd.

A CIP catalogue record for this book is available
from the British Library.

Printed in China by Imago

Papers used by Nosy Crow are made from
wood grown in sustainable forests.

1 3 5 7 9 8 6 4 2